Viz Graphic Novel

FLAME OF RECCA ™

Vol. 9
Story & Art by Nobuyuki Anzai

Contents

Flame of Recca
Vol. 9
Gollancz Manga Edition

Story and Art by
Nobuyuki Anzai

English Adaptation/Lance Caselman
Translation/Joe Yamazaki
Touch-Up & Lettering/Kelle Han
Graphics & Cover Design/Sean Lee
Editor/Yuki Takagaki
UK Cover Adaptation/Sue Michniewicz

© 1995 Nobuyuki ANZAI/Shogakukan Inc. First published by
Shogakukan Inc. in Japan as 'Recca no Honoo'. English publi-
cation rights in United Kingdom arranged by Shogakukan Inc.
through VIZ Media, LLC, U.S.A., Tuttle-Mori Agency, Inc., Japan,
and Ed Victor Ltd., U.K. All rights reserved. This edition published in great Britain in 2007 by Gollancz Manga,
an imprint of the Orion Publishing Group, Orion House, 5
Upper St Martin's Lane, London WC2H 9EA, and a licensee of
VIZ Media, LLC.

1 3 5 7 9 10 8 6 4 2

The right of Nobuyuki Anzai to be identified as the author of
this work has been asserted by him in accordance with the
Copyright, Designs and Patents Act 1988.

A CIP catalogue record for this book is available from the
British Library

ISBN-13 978 0 57508 0 874

Printed and bound by GGP, Germany

PARENTAL ADVISORY
Flame of Recca is rated T+ for Teen Plus. Contains realistic
and graphic violence. Recommended for older teens
(16 and up).

The Orion Publishing Group's policy is to use papers that are
natural, renewable and recyclable products and made from
wood grown in sustainable forests. The logging and manu-
facturing processes are expected to conform to the environ-
mental regulations of the country of origin.

www.orionbooks.co.uk

THERE WERE STRONG MOTIVATIONS--

IN THIS TOURNA-MENT, YOU GET TO KEEP THE TALISMANS OF THOSE YOU DEFEAT.

KAGERŌ, MY MOTHER ...

IF I COULD GET A MADOGU TO BREAK THE SPELL OF ETERNAL LIFE, I COULD TURN MOM BACK TO NORMAL!

YANAGI SAKOSHITA, MY PRINCESS ...

IF WE LOST, THEY WOULD TAKE HER AWAY AS THEIR PRIZE.

Part Seventy-Eight: The Man from Circus

KLAK

KLAK

YAK
YAK

HERE, THE POWERFUL ARE OUR HONORED GUESTS.

WE MUST ACCOM- MODATE THEM ACCORD- INGLY.

WHAT A FANCY DINNER.

I FEEL SO OUT OF PLACE.

BLUP

DON'T KNOW 'EM, DON'T KNOW 'EM...

OW, NO STABBING !!

KRASH

WHAK

HEY!! GIVE IT BACK, YOU BIG FRANKEN-YETI!!

I'LL EAT IT!

CHUNK

GRRR GRRR

THERE BETTER NOT BE ANYTHING WEIRD IN THIS.

HOKAGE, LED BY RECCA, DEFEATED KU, URUHA-MABOROSHI AND URUHA-OTO, AND TOMORROW WILL MOVE ON TO ROUND 4.

THE THIRD DAY OF THE TOURNAMENT WAS OVER.

HOKAGE
KU
SHINRAKAI
URUHA-MABOROSHI
TEIJIN
URUHA-OTO
HANNO
VIPER
HIDO
CIRCUS

THE WHOLE TEAM FEELS THE TENSION IN THEIR GUTS.

BUT MANY POWERFUL OPPONENTS STAND IN THEIR WAY.

URUHA-MA, WHO BEAT URUHA-KUROGANE TODAY, IS A FORMIDABLE OBSTACLE.

HOKAGE	Ⓐ	Ⓒ	URUHA-RAI
CIRCUS			ELEKIBRAN
URUHA-MA			P.O.G.
KAIENTAI	Ⓑ	Ⓓ	URUHA-KURENAI

TWO MORE VICTORIES AND HOKAGE WILL FACE KUREI.

ONLY EIGHT TEAMS REMAIN!

MY LORD, I...

FORGIVE ME...

TWITCH

I HEAR YOU LOST TO HOKAGE TODAY...

NEON.

...

LOOK ME IN THE EYE WHEN I'M SPEAKING TO YOU.

IT'S ALL RIGHT. YOU'RE NOT HERE TO BE CHASTISED.

BUT THEY DEFEATED YOU AS WELL. HOKAGE HAS GROWN STRONG.

I'M ACTUALLY PLEASED. THEY NOT ONLY BEAT GENJURO...

AND BESIDES...

BUT HOW LONG CAN THEY SURVIVE?

HOKAGE WILL HAVE TO FACE... *THEM.*

IT WILL BE ALL THE MORE SATISFYING WHEN I CRUSH THEM.

TODAY, WHEN THEY...

THERE IS SOME-THING I MUST ASK YOU ABOUT THEM!

...REFERRING TO US?

NEON, ARE YOU...

ROAR

RAAARR

KASHAMARU

TSUKISHIRO

GASHAKURA

MAGENSHA

HOW LONG HAVE YOU BEEN IN THE ROOM!?

YOU...

WHAT!

I'M STUNNED THAT THE OTHER TWO URUHA TEAMS COULDN'T BEAT THEM.

WHY, YOU!!

BOUM

IN TRUTH...

...

BUT HOKAGE COULD WIN TOMORROW. CAN YOU DEFEAT THEM?

THIS IS BETTER THAN I EXPECTED.

BUT PLEASE ALLOW ME TO FINISH.

FORGIVE MY RUDENESS.

TMP

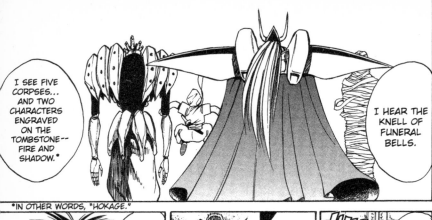

I SEE FIVE CORPSES... AND TWO CHARACTERS ENGRAVED ON THE TOMBSTONE-- FIRE AND SHADOW.*

I HEAR THE KNELL OF FUNERAL BELLS.

*IN OTHER WORDS, "HOKAGE."

JISHO WAS A GOOD MAN.

BUT EVEN GOOD WARRIORS FALL.

THEY KILLED OUR COMRADE JISHO.

YES ...

WERE YOU AWARE OF THAT, MASTER KUREI...?

AND, NEON...

WE WERE HERE FROM THE BEGINNING.

WHAM

THE PARK BEHIND THE HOTEL.

GRA...

...!!

MAGENSHA!!

BUT!!

HAVE YOU FORGOTTEN? URUHA IS ABOUT STRENGTH.

DO NOT BE SO QUICK TO JUDGE THEM.

TMP

HEY!! KEEP YOUR EYES CLOSED!!

FWP

WHY HAVE YOU BROUGHT ME HERE?

THIS IS GETTING WEIRD, DEAR...

...

RECCA?

? ? ? ?

YOU'RE AN ENEMY WHO WE SHOULD HATE, BUT...

THAT'S THE RULE! HERE, TAKE THE KOTO DAMA AND IDATEN.

KOTODAMA...

BONG...

I HOPE THESE WILL BE OF HELP TO YOU.

THIS MAY BE STRANGE, COMING FROM A MEMBER OF URUHA, BUT...

WE OWE YOU FOR SAVING SISTER NEON.

I DON'T WANT YOU TO HAVE TO WATCH ME GROW OLD!!

YOUR FRIENDS ALL TURNED INTO GEEZERS AND CRONES, BUT YOU STAYED YOUNG.

FOR FOUR HUNDRED YEARS YOU'VE STAYED YOUNG.

TWEEK

BUT...

IT'S NOT FAIR.

OKA, DO YOU SEE?

THIS IS OUR SON!

YOU'RE RIGHT...

LET'S GROW OLD TOGETHER...

I'LL MAKE THAT IDIOT KUREI PAY!!

I'LL REMOVE THAT CURSE FROM YOU! AND I WON'T LET THEM TAKE PRINCESS!!

MOM!! I'LL KEEP WINNING!!

I'VE GOT GOOD FRIENDS!!

DOMON, TOKIYA, FUKO, KAORU!!

WE'RE ALL GOING HOME TOGETHER!

BUT STILL CAME ALONG.

YOU GUYS HAVE NO CLASS SPYING ON THEM.

WHAT A STUBBORN ASS-WIPE!

...FOR ONCE I THOUGHT HE'D RELY ON HIS MOTHER.

AND KAORU

WOOO

URABUTOSATSUJIN, DAY 4

17

WHAT A SEXY MAN. ♪

BUT I'M ♥ A RECCA FAN!

WHAT AM I DOING?

OH.

...

HE'S BAD...

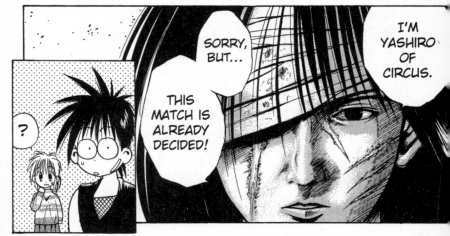

SORRY, BUT...

THIS MATCH IS ALREADY DECIDED!

I'M YASHIRO OF CIRCUS.

?

18

...OF CIRCUS.

SKRERSH!

SKRERSH!

I'M YASHIRO...

SKRERSH

SKRERSH!!

THIS MATCH IS OVER...

SORRY, BUT...

HE'S...

BAD!

WE LOSE.

...

CIRCUS MUST ...

FORFEIT.

Part Seventy-Nine:

The Vengeance Torch Is Passed

NO WAY!!

WHAT!

CANDY-ASS CHICKENS!!!

RAAAH

YOU GOTTA BE KIDDIN'!!

OOF!!

TO NK

WE WANNA SEE YOU KILL HOKAGE!!

WE WON'T LET YOU FORFEIT!!

BOO

BOO

THIS COULD TURN INTO A RIOT.

THE CROWD'S GETTING UGLIER.

C-CALM DOWN!

EEEK!

STOP THROWING THINGS!

WAK

FIGHT, PUSSY!!

JOE!?

FWOOSH

COWARD...

YOU GUTLESS...

22

I HELD BACK WITH THE FIRST BLAST, BUT NEXT TIME I WON'T.

IF YOU FEEL LUCKY, JUST LOOK INTO THE DRAGON'S EYE AND THROW SOMETHING.

ANYBODY WANT TO TRY ME?

YEAH, THAT'S SETSUNA ...

LOOKING INTO THAT DRAGON'S EYES MAKES YOU SPONTANEOUSLY COMBUST.

EEEK!

ACK ...

HE COULD'VE AT LEAST WARNED *US*.

NOT BAD.

LOOK AT THAT GOOSE-EGG!

GOOD JOB, RECCA!

(SETSU)

CALM DOWN OR YOU FRY!!

OKAY, NOW LET'S HEAR THE MAN OUT.

WHAT'S THE DEAL, YASHIRO?

WE ENTERED THIS TOURNAMENT...

WE WANTED REVENGE.

...FOR PERSONAL REASONS.

IT HAPPENED IN THAT TOURNAMENT...

...THE SECOND URABUTO-SATSUJIN!

SOME OF YOU MAY REMEMBER...

IT WAS FOUR YEARS AGO.

WU SP

WU SP

WE TOOK ONE CHARACTER FROM EACH OF OUR NAMES AND CAME UP WITH *CIRCUS.*

AND ME, YASHIRO.

GAIA... CHIGUSARI...

KARIN...

*IN JAPANESE, THE CHARACTERS CAN BE READ TOGETHER AS "CIRCUS."

RAAAAR

WE HAD ADVANCED FAIRLY EASILY UP TO THAT POINT.

CIRCUS — URUHA-KURENAI

BLOC B FINALS.

THEN!!

BUT...

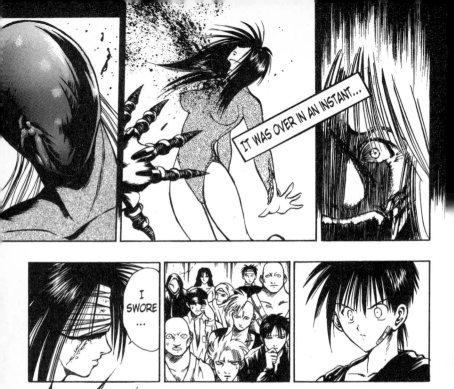

IT WAS OVER IN AN INSTANT...

I SWORE...

AND TAKE REVENGE !!!

I'LL NEVER FORGET THIS!!

ONE DAY, I WILL CHALLENGE YOU AGAIN...

YOU URUHA BASTARDS !!!

URUHA-KURENAI OVERWHELMED ITS OPPONENTS AND WON THE TOURNAMENT.

HE SMILED, THEN DISAPPEARED BEFORE OUR EYES.

HE ...

OUR QUEST FOR REVENGE BEGAN.

WE LOST A TEAMMATE, BUT OUR TEAM SPIRIT WAS STRONGER THAN EVER...

BUT NOW IT'S TIME FOR THE THIRD URABUTO-SATSUJIN!!

NOW I AM ALL THAT REMAINS OF TEAM CIRCUS.

THIS URABUTO-SATSUJIN IS MUCH TOUGHER THAN THE LAST ONE.

AS I DRAGGED THE COFFINS OF MY BELOVED TEAMMATES, I REALIZED...

BUT ...

GAIA WAS KILLED IN THE SECOND ROUND.

NOW ALL THE WEIGHT...IS ON YOUR SHOULDERS...

S-SORRY, YASHIRO ...

THEN CHIGUSARI WAS KILLED IN THE THIRD ROUND.

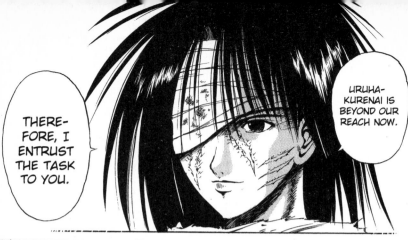

URUHA-KURENAI IS BEYOND OUR REACH NOW.

THERE-FORE, I ENTRUST THE TASK TO YOU.

DAT DON'T MEAN YA GOTTA FORFEIT...

SHUT UP!!

TO THE FIGHTERS OF...

HOKAGE!

YOU'VE SEEN HOKAGE IN ACTION...

YOU'VE GOT TO KNOW BY NOW...

IF ANYONE CAN BEAT KUREI'S TEAM...

IT'S YOU GUYS!

OF THE TWO TEAMS REMAINING IN BLOC A, ONE IS DOWN TO A LONE, DYING FIGHTER, WHILE EVERYBODY ON THE OTHER TEAM IS UNSCATHED.

TAKE THIS!!

THESE ARE WARRIORS OF RARE TALENT.

THEY'RE THE CHAMPIONS OF BLOC A!!

THEN WHY NOT GIVE THEM YOUR SUPPORT?

DO YOU SCUM THINK *YOU* CAN BEAT HOKAGE?

WE WANT THEM TO WIN, RIGHT!?

THEY REPRESENT *ALL* OF US!

RAAAAAH!

WE'RE GONNA WIN THE WHOLE THING !!!

WHAT ... WHAT ABOUT YOU?

I'M SORRY, PLEASE GIVE MY COMRADES A PROPER BURIAL.

TMP

HOKAGE WILL REPRESENT BLOC A!!!

HOKAGE VS. CIRCUS!! HOKAGE WINS ON A FORFEIT!!

I MUST GO...

GOT SOMEWHERE TO GO...

I HAVE... SOME- THING TO DO...

AM I A COWARD ...

GAIA, CHIGUSARI, KARIN...

RAAH

FUMP

NO WAY, YASHIRO!

...TO A BUNCH OF KIDS?

...FOR PASSING MY DUTY ON...

BUT NOW WE HAVE TO PASS THIS SACRED DUTY ON TO THOSE WHO ARE ABLE TO FULFILL IT.

WE NEVER RAN FROM OUR RESPONSIBILITY.

GAIA ...

THERE'S SOMETHING ABOUT THEM THAT MAKES ME BELIEVE IN THEM!

YOU DID THE RIGHT THING!

CHIGUSARI?

AFTER ALL, WE GOT TO MEET EACH OTHER AGAIN...

WHY DON'T WE REST NOW ...

THIS ISN'T...A DREAM IS IT...

...KARIN.

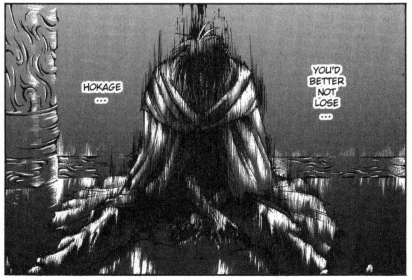

HOKAGE ...

YOU'D BETTER NOT LOSE ...

LOOK AT THOSE IDIOTS CHEERING THEM ON.

HMPH, I HEAR BLOC A HAD THE WEAKEST TEAMS, ANYWAY.

EVERYBODY'S CHEERING FOR 'EM.

BLOC B

HOKAGE'S GONNA REPRESENT BLOC A...

BELIEVING THEY WOULD BE VICTORIOUS.

THOSE WHO DIED ENTRUSTED THE SURVIVORS WITH THEIR HOPES...

LET'S FINISH UP BLOC B QUICKLY.

HOW NICE.

THEY WILL REPRESENT BLOC A!!

TEAM HOKAGE!
TOKIYA MIKAGAMI!
FUKO KIRISAWA!
KAORU KOGANEI!
DOMON ISHIJIMA!
RECCA HANABISHI!!!

DAY 4 OF THE URABUTO-SATSUJIN TOURNAMENT.

HOKAGE WINS ON A FORFEIT.

[BLOC A] HOKAGE VS. CIRCUS ...

!!

FWIP

...

Part Eighty: The Night Before

URUHA-MA WINS WITH 4 VICTORIES FOR GASHAKURA ...

[BLOC B] KAIENTAI VS. URUHA-MA...

URUHA-RAI WINS IN A CLEAN FIGHT.

[BLOC C] URUHA-RAI VS. ELEKIBRAN...

THIS WAS THE DAY REPRESENTATIVES OF ALL FOUR BLOCS WOULD BE DECIDED.

2 MINUTES 11 SECONDS INTO THE MATCH, FIVE MEMBERS OF P.O.G. WERE NO LONGER COUNTED AMONG THE LIVING.

[BLOC D] P.O.G. VS. URUHA-KURENAI ...

HOKAGE

DOMON

TOKIYA

FUKO

KAORU

RECCA HANABISHI
TEAM LEADER

THE TOP 4 ARE
DECIDED! ALL
THE TEAMS
BUT HOKAGE
ARE URUHA!!

THEY ARE THE
FIGHTING ELITE!
THEIR STRENGTH
OVERWHELMS
ALL OPPONENTS.

URUHA-RAI

RAIHA
(ONE-MAN TEAM)

GASHAKURA

MAGENSHA
TEAM LEADER

KASHAMARU TSUKISHIRO

URUHA-MA

Part Eighty:
The Night Before

URUHA-KURENAI

(?)   (?)   (MIKOTO)

NOROI

KUREI
TEAM LEADER

SOUNDS MORE LIKE STUPIDITY THAN CONFIDENCE.

I DUNNO. I WAS TAKING A NAP.

SWUFF

SLURP

SLURP

RECREATION ROOM

THEN WHO BESIDES URUHA-MA ADVANCED?

IT'S KAORU AND SAICHO. WHAT A GRUESOME TWOSOME.

HEY!

HEY! PUDDING-SHAKE!! YOU WANT ONE?

HUH?

CHOMP

OKAY, THEN ...

READY?

BUMP

BUMP

BUMP

HUFF

HUFF

HA HA

YOU'RE AMAZING, SAICHO.

IF ONLY RECCA HAD A TALENT ...

AWE- SOME!

LOOK! TWO SECONDS FLAT!

WELL ...

WHOA!!

POOF

42

HER NAME WAS MISORA.

HUFF HUFF HUFF

YOU BONELESS CHICKEN !!

CAN'T WE...TAKE A TINY BREAK?

HUFF HUFF HUFF

FUKO...

THAT'S MEAN...

YOU'LL NEVER FIND A GIRL THE WAY YOU ARE.

AHHH, YOU'RE SO REFRESHINGLY DIRECT!!

...

UH-OH, IS HE MAD THAT I HIT HIM!?

FROM THE...

Y-YOU'RE...

HE HASN'T FIGURED OUT THAT I HIT HIM?

WHAT A MORON...

I WAS VERY DISAP-POINTED.

I WAS MYSTERIOUSLY KNOCKED UNCONSCIOUS. AND WHEN I AWOKE, YOU WERE GONE.

THE DAY BEFORE YESTERDAY WAS QUITE A DAY.

MY NAME IS RAIHA.

YIKES !!

BUT WE MEET AGAIN !

MY NAME'S RAIHA!

HELLO! NICE TO MEET YOU!

HANDS OFF MY GODDESS, PEE-WEE!

SHUP

OH, LOOKING FOR TROUBLE, EH!?

WHAT A STRANGE MOVE, LIKE A LEAF FLOATING ON THE BREEZE...

WHAT THE HECK?

KLANK

!

WIP

DOMON, RIGHT?

I HOPE I DIDN'T OFFEND YOU.

I'M SORRY. I CAN BE A LITTLE TOO FAMILIAR SOMETIMES.

MISS FUKO, LET'S GO ON A DATE SOON.

WELL THEN, GOODBYE.

KISS MY BIG ROTATING --!!

CHEATING!?

FUKO!! ARE YOU CHEATING ON ME!?

I JUST MET THE GUY!!

THAT WAS A POWERFUL PUNCH, BUT BIG MOVEMENTS LIKE THAT ARE EASY TO EVADE.

A SHORTER SWING AND MORE HIP ROTATION MIGHT SERVE YOU BETTER.

"LET'S GO ON A DATE SOON."

"MISS FUKO..."

...

HOW...

DOES HE KNOW MY NAME?

!

HE'S KIND OF PRETTY, BUT NOT HANDSOME LIKE ME.

HE'S NO THREAT!

HMPH!

...

HUH?

...

WHO IS HE?

RAIHA, HUH? HE DOESN'T SEEM LIKE A BAD GUY...

SHE DIDN'T THINK MUCH OF TEAM KU.

MISORA WAS MASTER KUKAI'S ONLY DAUGHTER...

IT'S NO FUN! AND EVERYONE THINKS I'M A SISSY!

KLAK

ARGH!! I GET A NEW SCAR EVERYDAY IN TRAINING!

WAP

SAICHO!

WHY DON'T YOU QUIT KU!

IT'S NOT REALLY YOUR THING.

WE WERE BLESSED WITH A GIRL, AND ONE THAT HATES FIGHTING TO BOOT.

WHAT TO DO...

AND NOW IF YOU QUIT, KU'S LEGACY WILL END...

DON'T FEEL TOO BAD.

HA HA! IS THAT WHAT MY CRAZY DAUGHTER SAID!?

HA HA HA, DON'T BE EMBAR-RASSED!

I WISH YOU WOULD MARRY MISORA.

REALLY FOND OF SAICHO.

KAORU'S ...

HEE HEE HEE

OH, OKAY, OKAY!

HELP ME, SAICHO!

WHAK

SHUT UP!!

I'LL BURN YOU, DAMN IT!!

POW

BAM

NOW THAT WAS PROFOUND! SO DIFFERENT FROM RECCA.

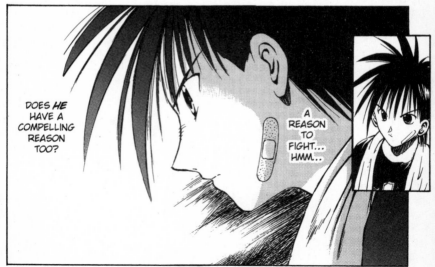

DOES *HE* HAVE A COMPELLING REASON TOO?

A REASON TO FIGHT... HMM...

KUREI...

SOON IT WILL ALL REACH FRUITION.

HEH HEH... EVERYTHING IS GOING ACCORDING TO PLAN.

HRUMB

THE MAIN PLAYERS WILL ASSEMBLE SOON.

HEH HEH

HEH HA

HA HA HA HA HA HA HA HA !!

AND...

I, MORI KŌRAN...

KUREI...

RECCA...

THE HEALING GIRL, YANAGI SAKOSHITA...

BLUP

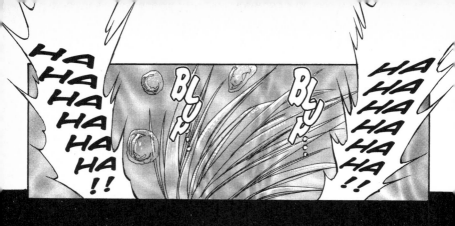

THE WHEELS HAVE
BEGUN TO TURN.

THEY CANNOT BE
CHANGED...

THE WHEELS
OF *DESTINY*.

THEY CANNOT BE
ESCAPED...

THEY CANNOT BE
FATHOMED...

54

Part Eighty-One:
The Time of Mara* (1) Moon

THE THIRD URABUTOSATSUJIN SEMI-FINAL MATCH (GROUP 1)

URUHA-MA   HOKAGE

*IN BUDDHISM, MARA (OR GOUMA) IS THE PERSSONIFICATION OF EVIL.

THE FIFTH DAY--

I WANT TO DO IT!!

ZODIAC DRESSING ROOM

A REFEREE HAS TO BE IMPARTIAL.

COME ON, TATSUKO...

INUKO (DOG)

DRAGON TATSUKO

I'VE SWORN TO SEE HOKAGE THROUGH TO THE END!!

SHAKE

UMI (RABBIT)

NEMI (OX)

DUH

I THINK URUHAMA HAS AN ADVANTAGE.

YOKO (SHEEP)

56

A POPU-LARITY POLL!!

WHAT'S THAT!?

ROCK PAPER SCISSORS !?

NO! TATSUKO'S UNCANNILY GOOD AT THAT!!

WE'LL CHANGE REFS FOR EACH FIGHT!!

ALL RIGHT, HOW ABOUT THIS?

HUFF

HUFF

IT'S ABOUT WHICH OF THEM WILL REF TODAY'S FIGHTS.

WHAT ARE THEY FIGHTING ABOUT?

GRR

YIP

RARR

STAFF

OKAY !!

AND SO THE SEMI-FINALS BEGAN.

A NEW FIGHTING FLOOR WAS INSTALLED IN THE ARENA.

I CAN'T KEEP UP...

TATSUKO, LEAVE YOUR FEELINGS FOR RECCA OUT OF THIS!

I'LL REF RECCA'S FIGHT!

57

ARENA E

THEY'RE KEYED UP ALL RIGHT.

I HOPE WE WON'T HAVE ANOTHER RIOT.

WHAT WAS THAT, BLOC B!?

I DARE YOU TO SAY THAT AGAIN!!

HMPH!! THEY'RE JUST THE DREGS OF WIMPY OLD BLOC A!!

WHY'S TOKIYA OVER THERE?

UM, QUESTION--

I'M SITTING OUT TODAY. I'M STILL RECOVERING FROM OUR MATCH WITH OTO.

I HAVE TO SAVE MYSELF FOR THE FINALS TOMORROW.

FWUMP

COMMENTATOR

ACTUALLY...

STOP SCREWING AROUND!!

I INVITED HIM TO. I'M A BIG FAN!

I EVEN GOT HIS AUTO-GRAPH!

I THOUGHT I'D WATCH HOKAGE OBJEC-TIVELY FOR ONCE...

YOU'RE GOING TO BE A COMMEN-TATOR?

BLUSH

Nemi, best wishes.

Tokiya Mikagami

CAN'T COMPLAIN SINCE HE GOT IN A FIGHT WITH OTO DURING THAT MATCH.

OKAY, THEN...

BUT...

THAT HURTS US.

SO TOKIYA'S NOT FIGHTING TODAY.

JEALOUS, EH?

WHAM

DIE, YOU!!

HE MUST HAVE CONFI-DENCE IN US, RIGHT?

WHO NEEDS HIM!?

OH, WELL...

RAAH

!!

NOW ENTERING FROM CORNER B, URUHA-MA!!

TO

KLANG

...

KLANG

戈

ME

INUKO GETS TO REF THE FIRST FIGHT AFTER ALL.

TWO OF ME!!?

ACK!

YEAH.

CREEPY.

WHOOM

BOO!

SLORX

GASP

URUHA NINJA...

KASHAMARU!
(FIRE WHEEL)

TRANS-FORMATION TECHNIQUE--

WOW! WHAT AN ENTRANCE !!!

RAAAH

HOKAGE'S DEAD MEAT!!

HE LOOKS TOUGH!!

BRASSIERE !!

KLAP

KLAP

DUDE, IT'S "BRAVO" ...

HEH HEH...

THERE WERE MOUTHY MEN LIKE YOU IN BLOC B, TOO.

FANCY ENTRANCES AND COSTUMES MEAN DIDDLY-SQUAT TO ME.

MAYBE YOU'D BE BETTER OFF WITH A RABBIT AND A HAT?

THEY'RE DEAD NOW.

URABUTOSATSUJIN SEMI-FINALS (GROUP 1) TEAMS

—— HOKAGE ——	—— URUHA-MA ——
 KAORU KOGANEI	 TSUKISHIRO
 RECCA HANABISHI	 KASHAMARU
 FUKO KIRISAWA	 GASHAKURA
 DOMON ISHIJIMA	 MAGENSHA

HE DOESN'T LOOK AS STRONG AS THEY SAY.

SO HE'S THE URUHA TRAITOR KOGANEI.

HEH...

HEH HEH

THAT THE PREDICTION WAS NO EMPTY BOAST.

WELL, WHEN HE SEES WHAT TSUKISHIRO CAN DO, HE'LL REALIZE...

FWUP

BEGIN!!!

RUNNING WILD

WORRY ABOUT THAT LATER!! FIGHT!!!

AM I THAT COCKY?

HMM, DO I REALLY COME ACROSS LIKE THAT?

74

Part Eighty-Two:

The Time of Mara (2)

Crescent Moon

TSUKISHIRO
VS.
KOGANE!!!

BEGIN
!!!

AND YOU LOOK KINDA WEAK.

I WON'T NEED *THAT* JUST YET...

KLINK...

THIS SHOULD BE ENOUGH.

IT HAS THAT SHAPE ...

BUT IT FUNCTIONS MORE LIKE A SWORD.

IS IT A BOOMERANG?

AN ODD WEAPON, ISN'T IT, MR. MIKAGAMI?

GRRR ...

OR THE *TULWAR* USED ON THE INDIAN SUB-CONTINENT.

A BLADE DESIGNED FOR SLICING PEOPLE.

THE EXTREMELY CURVED BLADE IS RATHER LIKE THE S-SHAPED ETHIOPIAN *SHOTEL*...

WHOOM

HIS SWORD'S JUST A BLUR!!

WHOA!!!

AND THAT KOGANEI KID ISN'T HALF BAD!!

!

PROUD TO FIGHT FOR HOKAGE, EH?

!

YEAH!! HOKAGE'S KAMIKAZE FIGHTER!!

GGOO?!

KICK HIS ASS!!

I DON'T KNOW ANY OF YOU GUYS.

YOU KNOW ABOUT ME?

BUT YOU ONCE FOUGHT FOR KUREI.

CLEARLY, YOUR HEART NO LONGER BELONGS TO URUHA.

THAT'S NOT SURPRISING.

EVEN AMONG THE URUHA, ONLY A HANDFUL OF PEOPLE KNOW OF OUR EXISTENCE.

KASHAMARU...

GASHAKURA...

TSUKISHIRO...

WE ARE *URA-URUHA*-- THE DARK SIDE.

...AND MAGENSHA!

URUHA!?

URA--

WE FINALLY GET TO LEARN WHO THEY ARE.

SO.

NEON ...

THE DIVISION CAN ARISE NATURALLY ...

OR BE CREATED WITH GREAT DELIBERATION.

WE ARE THE LATTER CASE...

IN ANY LARGE ORGANIZATION, THERE IS THE FACE THE WORLD SEES--AND THE HIDDEN, DARK SIDE.

TO COUNTER THAT...

THERE IS URA-URUHA!

THE POSSIBILITY OF A REBELLIOUS CELL EMERGING INCREASES.

THE MORE PEOPLE INVOLVED, THE MORE INDIVIDUAL MINDS AND AMBITIONS THERE ARE.

A CANCER CAN DEVELOP, EVEN WITHIN URUHA.

NEON KILLED THE REBEL GENJURO FOR US, BUT...

WE'VE CARVED MANY CANCEROUS FOOLS FROM THE FLESH OF URUHA.

NOW THAT WE'RE HERE ON THE OUTSIDE...

ALL WHO'VE OPPOSED MASTER KUREI...

WE'RE A KIND OF SECRET INTERNAL HIT SQUAD FOR THE URUHA ASSASSINS.

TRAITOR.

WE WILL DISPOSE OF YOU OUR-SELVES...

HEH

URUHA IS A COVERT ORGANIZATION.

AND WE ARE FAR MORE SECRET STILL.

86

JUST AS I PREDICTED.

I'VE WON WITHOUT MY OPPONENT EVER TOUCHING ME.

DO YOU KNOW WHY?

OOOOO

HA HA ...

FUMP

IMAGINE IF THIS BEAUTIFUL FACE OF MINE WERE SCARRED.

I LIKE BEING CLEAN. I DON'T LET ANYONE TOUCH ME.

THIS FIGHT'S OVER, DOGGIE.

WATCH THE MOUTH, JERK.

I HATE 'EM!!

WHAT DO YOU THINK OF HIS TYPE, YANAGI?

GREAT, A HOMICIDAL NARCISSIST.

88

OF COURSE NOT!! WE BEAT EACH OTHER UP ALL THE TIME!

YOU SHOULDN'T PICK ON KAORU SO MUCH...

TSUKISHIRO PUNCHES HARD, BUT HE DID LITTLE DAMAGE TO THE RUNT!

HMM.. WONDERFUL.

YOU'RE SMALL SO CONFUSE THE ENEMY...

STEP INTO IT!

NO!

I WAS TRAINED...

...BY KUREI, TOO...

KLAK

PLUP

TUMP

...

90

91

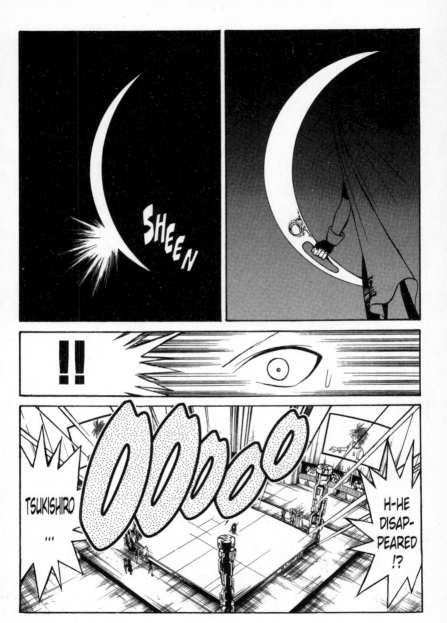

92

WHAT THE HELL'S GOING ON!?

TSUKISHIRO WAVED HIS SASH...

HEH HEH... YOU CAN'T SEE ME.

WHERE CAN I BE?

IN FRONT OF YOU? OR BESIDE YOU... HEH...

THAT SASH...

...IS AN OBORO.

THE CRESCENT MOON OBSCURED BY CLOUDS IN THE DARKNESS OF NIGHT.

IT IS A MADOGU OF INVISIBILITY!!

94

Part Eighty-Three:
The Time of Mara(3)
Lunar Eclipse

96

SHIT
...

THAT WAS CLOSE !!

WHOA ...

HE'S A LUCKY ONE.

SENSING THE ATTACK FROM THE BLOOD...

BUT HOW LONG CAN HIS LUCK LAST?

TURNING INVISIBLE SHOULD BE AGAINST THE RULES! IT'S NOT FAIR!!

THAT'S NOT COOL!

YOU'RE STRONGER THAN THAT!!

DON'T GIVE UP!!

BUT HOW CAN I SEE THROUGH IT?

TRY TO SEE THROUGH HIS TRICK!

...

YEAH, A MAN DOESN'T WIMP OUT!

IDIOTS!!
(TIMES 3)

A SIXTH SENSE!

YOUR MIND'S EYE!

OUIJA BOARD!

I KNOW!! I KNOW!

MUMBLE MUMBLE

UH-HUH UH-HUH

RIGHT?

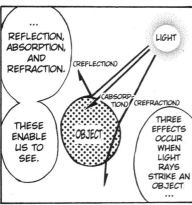

...REFLECTION, ABSORPTION, AND REFRACTION.

LIGHT

(REFLECTION)

(ABSORP-TION)

(REFRACTION)

OBJECT

THESE ENABLE US TO SEE.

THREE EFFECTS OCCUR WHEN LIGHT RAYS STRIKE AN OBJECT. ...

IF THOSE EFFECTS ARE SOMEHOW BLOCKED...

MATTER CANNOT BE SEEN!

DO YOU KNOW ABOUT OPTICS?

BEING ABLE TO SEE OBJECTS IS ENABLED BY THE REACTION OF LIGHT ON MATTER.

FWUP

THAT'S OBORO'S POWER!!

TO WEAKEN THE REFRACTION TO THE POINT OF INVISIBILITY...

DIS-APPEARS!!

UH, TSUKISHIRO ONCE AGAIN...

THAT'S NOT GOOD ...

KOGANEI LOOKS LIKE HE'S LOSING IT!!

WOOSH

WHY ...

YOU!!

WOOSH

SHUNK

STOP FLAILING, KAORU !!

YOU'LL TIRE YOURSELF OUT!!

BUT ...

WHAT ELSE CAN I DO?

GLURP

FROM BEHIND!!?

GRUP

GET UP.

NOT YET...

I DID NOT STRIKE TO KILL.

UNH...

HIS BACK'S BEEN CUT!!!

IS HE DEAD!?

IS HE...

I DESPISE IGNORANT CLODS... HEH HEH HEH.

YOU DIDN'T UNDERSTAND MY EXPLANATION OF REFRACTION, DID YOU?

AND IT FORE-SHADOWED WHAT WAS TO COME.

THAT'S WHY I MADE MY ENTRANCE WRAPPED IN BANDAGES. I WAS USING THEM AS A MOTIF.

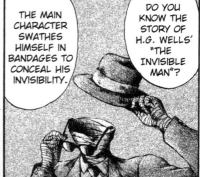

THE MAIN CHARACTER SWATHES HIMSELF IN BANDAGES TO CONCEAL HIS INVISIBILITY.

DO YOU KNOW THE STORY OF H.G. WELLS' "THE INVISIBLE MAN"?

SWAPP

BUT IT WAS LOST ON AN UNEDUCATED CHIMP LIKE YOU.

104

KAORU'S NOT FINISHED YET.

PRINCESS ...

UNH ...

TIME OUT.

W UP

SHA TWAK

WHAM

UH-OH, THAT'S NO GOOD!

THIS IS TOO ONE-SIDED.

BUT ...

BUT ...

THE LITTLE GUY MUST BE PRETTY PISSED OFF NOW.

AND TO TAKE A BEATING FROM A FOE WHO BRAGS BECAUSE HE SHOWED UP AT SCHOOL A FEW TIMES.

THE TARGET IS MARKED.

BUT THE NEXT TIME HE DISAPPEARS IS YOUR OPPORTUNITY!

NOW, NOW, DON'T CRY PRETTY GIRL!!

UM... YOU'RE JOKER, RIGHT?

WUP

HE'S PRANCING AROUND,* SAYING "I'M INVISIBLE, I'M INVISIBLE!"

*USES AN EXPRESSION FROM THE KANSAI DIALECT.

IF YOU HAVE THE STONES,

TRY YOUR PET INVISIBLE-MAN TRICK AGAIN.

♪ HEH HEH. THEN TRY IT AGAIN.

TARGET?

YOUR BULLSHIT WON'T WORK ON ME, FOOL.

WHAT DID YOU SAY?

BLAME THAT HARLEQUIN FOR GETTING YOU KILLED, BOY.

I'M ONLY THE ONE WHO GOT A REQUEST FOR MURDER.

FWUP

SHEEN

OBORO...

UNNNGH!!!

SPLURP

BUT H-HOW!?

I WAS... INVISIBLE...

PEACE.

SPLAK

"THE TRICK-STER FALLS VICTIM TO HIS OWN TRICK." IF THERE'S COLOR ON THE TALISMAN THAT HIDES THE JUTSUSHA...

IT'S NOT SO EFFECTIVE.

THE TARGET WAS KAORU'S OWN BLOOD ON THE OBORO!!

PUMMELING KAORU CAME BACK TO BITE HIS ASS!

POW KRAK WHAM THWAK WHAM KA-BAM BAM THWAK

LOOKS LIKE HE'S READY FOR THE BANDAGES MOTIF AGAIN!!

HA HA

HE OVERDID IT...

EDUCATED GENTLE-MAN OR NOT, YUCK...

FsSs Fsss Fsss

WHAT A WASTE OF A HANDSOME GUY. ♡

I HATE PANSIES.

PSYCH.

YOU DON'T KNOW THE MEANING OF "NEVER GIVE UP," DO YOU?

KAORU !!

Part Eighty-Four:

The Time of Mata (4)
Ninja Battle

KAORU!!!

TMP

YOU ALL RIGHT!? SAY SOME-THING!!

STOP BRAGGING!! HAVE YOU LOOKED IN THE MIRROR LATELY?

WOOOOOHO!

THERE'S NO WAY HE'S FINE AFTER FIGHTING ME.

IT'S N-NOTHING... NOTHING AT ALL...

HEH HEH... I'M FINE...

I'LL TAKE HIM TO THE INFIRMARY.

WHAT'S WORRYING YOU?

DON'T EVEN THINK ABOUT TOUCHING HER.

INFIRMARY... PLEASE...?

BUMP BUMP

YANAGI, WILL YOU COME ALONG AND HEAL HIM?

DON'T WORRY, HE'S EXHAUSTED, BUT HIS WOUNDS AREN'T DEEP.

TOKIYA...

SURE.

LORD MAGENSHA, WHAT ARE YOU...?

WHAT?

THIS MATCH...

RUNNING WILD.

HMPH... I KNEW WE SHOULDN'T HAVE USED THAT FOOL.

NO...

HE DID WELL FOR ONE OF HIS LEVEL.

IS A DRAW !!!

RRAAAAAH

WHAT !!?

AS THE UMPIRE...

AS YOU ALREADY KNOW FROM THE URUHA-OTO MATCH, THERE'S A PENALTY WHEN TEAM-MATES INTER-FERE IN A FIGHT!

FOR INSTANCE, PICKING UP A FALLEN FIGHTER IS PROHIBITED UNTIL THE OUTCOME OF THE MATCH HAS BEEN DECLARED!!

WILD

GRP...

WHADDYA MEAN? THE FIGHT WAS OBVIOUSLY--

THOSE ARE THE RULES!!

WELL DONE!!

EVERYONE HERE KNOWS WHO WON THE FIGHT.

STILL ...

KOGANEI !!!

YAAAAY

KOGANEI !!

KOGANEI !!

NOT REALLY ...

I HARDLY SAID ANYTHING.

YOUR HINT SAVED HIM.

THANKS, JOKER.

118

KSSH

REFEREE OF
2ND MATCH

T I
A N
T U
S K
U O
K
O ←

KSSH

KSSH

THE
DRAGON
GIRL

HUH?

I'M SO
HAPPY!!
LUCKY
ME!!

HOKAGE'S
LEADER
--RECCA
HANABISHI
!!

CUR-
RENTLY
SIX FOR
SIX, UNDE-
FEATED,
AND
RANKED
SECOND
OVERALL
!!

AND HERE
HE IS!!
THE
BACKBONE
OF TEAM
HOKAGE
!!

AND...

RAAAH

THE AUDIENCE
IS NEARING A
FEVER PITCH!!
HE CARRIES
THE HOPES
AND DREAMS
OF BLOC A ON
HIS SHOUL-
DERS!!!

REPRESENTING
URUHA-MA...

THESE SAME
MEN WERE
BOOING HIM A
FEW DAYS AGO!
HOW FICKLE
THEY ARE--ALL
OF THEM!!

120

123

124

AND THAT WAS "NINPO *UTSUSEMI" (EMPTY CICADA MANEUVER)

YOU EXPECT ME TO BELIEVE YOU'RE A NINJA? YOU'RE 10,000 LIGHT YEARS FROM THAT!!

TRYING TO PASS YOURSELF OFF AS MY MASTER, EH? INEXCUS-ABLE!!

*TO SUBSTITUTE SOMEONE FOR ONESELF TO ESCAPE INJURY.

SKREFFF

DARN, I GOT STARTED LATE.

THE SECOND MATCH HAS BEGUN!!

I'M STILL A NINJA FREAK TO THE BONE! ♡

IT FELT GOOD TO DO THAT OLD MOVE AGAIN.

LIKE YOU'VE EVER TOUCHED 'EM...

FIRST OF ALL, PRINCESS'S BREASTS AREN'T THAT BIG!!

BWAH HA HA HA

I'M GONNA TELL ON YOU LATER.

SWIK

HEH HEH! THIS IS GOING TO BE GOOD.

A NINJA BATTLE!

THAT KID IS IN FOR A SHOCK...

FINE.

AND IF I WIN, I'LL RIP THAT NINJA PLAYSUIT OFF OF YOU!

LET'S SEE IF YOU STILL ARE AFTER THIS MOVE!

KLK

YOU'RE VERY SURE OF YOURSELF, BUT...

... WHEN HE SEES KASHAMARU'S NINJUTSU.

... KAGAMI JIGOKU!!! (MIRROR HELL)

FWOOM

NINPO ...

SAIHA (SMASHED WING) --TYPE ONE
ARMS THE WIELDER WITH A BLADE OF FIRE. RECCA'S MOST COMMONLY USED DRAGON.

HOMURA (FLOCK OF FLAMES)--TYPE THREE
A WHIP-LIKE BELT OF FIRE FOR WHIPPING AND PUNCHING--AND MANY OTHER USES.

MADOKA (RING)--TYPE FIVE
KING OF THE FLAMING FORCE FIELD. THE FLAME SPHERE GENERATED BY ITS THREE EYES CREATES A FORCE FIELD.

NADARE (AVALANCHE) --TYPE TWO
GENERATES NUMEROUS FIREBALLS. HAS THE MOST PEACEFUL PERSONALITY.

SETSUNA (MOMENT) --TYPE SEVEN
WHEN SETSUNA'S SINGLE EYE OPENS, ITS SHUN-EN INCINERATES ALL WHO SEE IT. CRUEL AND FEROCIOUS.

Part Eighty-Five:
The Time of Mara (5) Eight-Dragon Battle

130

破羅羅
HARA (SCROLL)
OF DESTRUCTION

THE HACHIRYU CAN ONLY BE USED BY ONE WHO HAS...

...THE BLOOD OF THE HOKAGE CLAN LEADERS !!!

YOUR BEST MOVE, THE FLAME OF YAMATA, NO LONGER BELONGS ONLY TO YOU.

NADARE SAI HO SETSU MADOKA

I, TOO, CAN WIELD IT.

DRAGON FLAME TYPE TWO-- NADARE !!!

SHBOM

SWUP

LOOK!

KASHAMARU CAN DO IT, TOO!!?

HEY!! ISN'T THAT RECCA'S MOVE!?

HOW CAN KASHAMARU USE THE HACHIRYU!?

NO WAY!!!

DAMN!!

SKREEE

IT'S NOT ONLY NADARE HE CONTROLS.

SURPRISED ALREADY?

!!

ZA...

!!

SHINK

UNH
...

PLURT

COULD THIS BE A HUGE UPSET!?

THEY'RE EVENLY MATCHED!!

THERE IS SOME DECEPTION GOING ON!! ONLY, RECCA CAN WIELD THE DRAGON FLAMES!

IMPOSSIBLE!

!!

KUNOICHI.
(FEMALE NINJA)

HEH HEH...
SO YOU
NOTICED...

THE
NISE-BI--
THE
FALSE
FLAME!!

THE FIRE-
MAKING
MADOGU...

EVENTUALLY,
THAT DESIRE
WAS APPEASED
THROUGH
BLACK MAGIC...

ENJUTSUSHI-
FIRE WIELDER-
THE TITLE BORNE
ONLY BY THE
LEADER OF THE
HOKAGE, WAS
COVETED BY ALL
SHINOBI.

IN THE
FORM OF
THE NISE-BI
TALISMAN!!

(FIRE)

TEAM URUHA-KURENAI, IT IS TIME.

TRUE, A NISE-BI ALONE CAN'T WIELD THE HACHIRYU.

EXCEPT WHEN THE SORCERER IS KASHAMARU, AS YOU HAVE SEEN.

BUT IT WAS A POOR IMITATION!!

THE FLAME WAS NOTHING COMPARED TO THAT OF AN ENJUTSU-SHI!

AND THE EIGHT DRAGONS OF THE NISE-BI WOULD BE PALTRY REFLECTIONS!

I'VE SEEN ALL OF YOUR MOVES!!

YEAH.

CREEPY.

TRUE, I AM A SKILLED MIMIC! AND I USE THAT TO MY ADVANTAGE.

AND I CAN IMITATE ANY MOVE AFTER SEEING IT ONLY ONCE!

FSSSS

YOU CALLED ME A NINJA-MIMICKING MONKEY, RECCA.

SAIHA!!

SLISH

TUMP

LIKE THIS ONE!!

HFF NO...

WAY...

F-NUMP

UNGH!!

HE'S IN SHOCK FROM SEEING THE HACHIRYU USED AGAINST HIM.

HE'S LOST HIS WILL TO FIGHT!

THIS ISN'T GOOD...

PULL YOURSELF TOGETHER, RECCA!!

...THINKS SO HIGHLY OF THIS PUNK IS BEYOND ME.

WHY MASTER KUREI...

MAKE AN EXAMPLE OF HIM TO BLOC A!!

YEAH, FINISH HIM OFF!!

GYA HA HA

141

WHO WAS THAT?

WHAT?

I ASK YOU...

A LONG TIME AGO, THERE WAS A TALENTED WRITER WHO, AFTER MANY YEARS, WROTE A STORY...

!

THE WRITER SAID, "THIS IS MY STORY!"

THE FORGER ALSO SAID, "THIS IS MY STORY."

BUT THAT STORY WAS COPIED BY ANOTHER MAN AND THERE WERE NOW TWO OF THE SAME STORY IN THE WORLD.

WHO *ARE* YOU!?

HE CAN COPY ALL THAT HE HAS SEEN, BUT HE CANNOT COPY WHAT HE HAS NOT SEEN!!

IF YOU KNOW THE ANSWER, THEN DO THE SAME!

A NEW KARYU!

IT HAS SHOWN ITSELF...

!!!

I GIVE POWER TO THOSE WHO CAN ANSWER MY RIDDLE!!

I AM RUI, THE SHAPELESS ONE!!

I WILL NOT ALLOW YOU TO SURRENDER, KASHAMARU...

YOU ARE URA-URUHA!

I WILL PUNISH YOU IF YOU DISHONOR US.

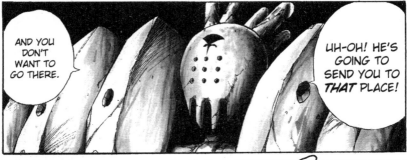

AND YOU DON'T WANT TO GO THERE.

UH-OH! HE'S GOING TO SEND YOU TO *THAT* PLACE!

BUT THAT'S...!?

SHUDOOO

B-BUT...

Part Eighty-Six: The Time of Mara (6) Howl of The Shapeless One

Part Eighty-Six:

The Time of Mara (6)

Howl of The Shapeless One

RUI!

ALL RIGHT, I'LL TRY!

WOOOSH

FOG ...

IT'S POURING OUT OF RECCA'S BODY!!

WHAT'S GOING ON!!?

WHOA!!

FWOOOO

153

154

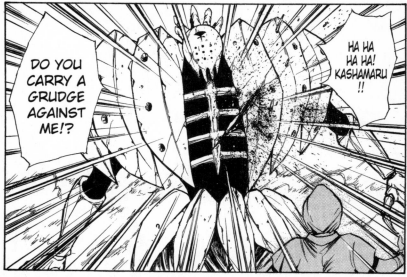

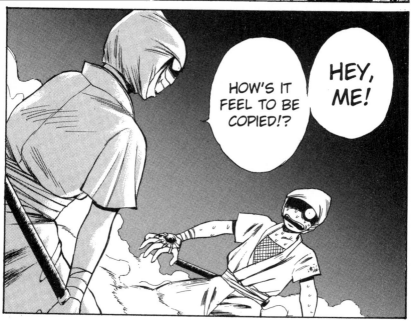

MY SWORD...

IT'S GONE!!

!

AND *THIS* WAS SAIHA!!

SH.NK

PLAIN GUNPOWDER BALLS IGNITED BY THE NISE-BI!

THESE WERE YOUR NADARE'S FIREBALLS, EH?

BUT YOU'RE STILL GREEN ENOUGH TO HAVE THE SECRET OF YOUR POWERS REVEALED.

I WISH I COULD SAY YOU ARE A TRUE NINJA...

YOU DISGUISED YOUR SWORD AND WHIP WITH THE NISE-BI, SO IT APPEARED THAT YOU CONTROLLED FIRE DRAGONS!

YOU EVEN CONJURED AN IMAGE OF A KARYU.

FWOOO

THE FOG IS BLOCKING OUR VIEW!!

WHAT'S GOING ON IN THERE!!?

WHAT'S...

...

UNH...

WAP

DO NOT TAKE THE HACHIRYU LIGHTLY ...

POWER

AND I UNDERSTAND RUI'S POWER !!!

I-I KNOW WHO YOU ARE !!

I WILL CHANGE MY FORM AS YOU WILL ME TO...

GUIDE MY POWERS WITH YOUR MIND!

RUI TOLD ME THIS...

HA HA HA HA HA HA HA

THAT IS RYU-NO-EN ROKU-SHIKI!!! (DRAGON FLAME TYPE SIX)--RUI!!

THE FLAME TOOK THE SHAPE OF WHATEVER I IMAGINED, OBJECT OR BEING!

HEY, ME!

HOW'S IT FEEL TO BE COPIED!?

TAKE MY ADVICE. IF YOU COME AT ME AGAIN, I WON'T HOLD BACK!!

JUST GIVE UP! YOU CAN'T POSSIBLY FIGHT ME IN THAT CONDITION.

I CAN'T DISOBEY THOSE TWO...

CHITTER

CHITTER

HEH HEH...I WISH I COULD TAKE YOUR ADVICE, BUT...

BLOC A CAMP

YOU'RE THE BEST !!!

RAARRR

I KNEW YOU'D DO IT, BOSS!!

HE WAS AFRAID OF BEING SENT TO SOME PLACE.

BUT KASHAMARU SEEMED ODDLY FRIGHTENED OF SOMETHING!

THIS IS YOUR SIXTH HACHIRYU. THE DAY WHEN YOU CAN WIELD ALL EIGHT IS NOT FAR OFF!

YOU WERE ALMOST FOOLED BY A GI-RYU, A FALSE DRAGON CREATED BY THE FALSE FLAME OF NISE-BI.

YAY!!

SWAK

KRANG

THE REAL MONSTER IS COMING UP!!

IT'S NOT OVER YET!

THE REAL TERROR OF URUHA-MA IS ABOUT TO BE REVEALED !!

SHIT! WHAT A LOSER!!

BLOC B CAMP

165

FWASH

OMELET
...

SHOOOO

KAORU.

YOU'RE
ALL
RIGHT
NOW...

PHEW!

ZZZZZ

Part Eighty-Seven: The Time of Mara(?)
Gashakura Enters the Battle

Part Eighty-Seven:
The Time of Mara (7)
Gashakura Enters the Battle

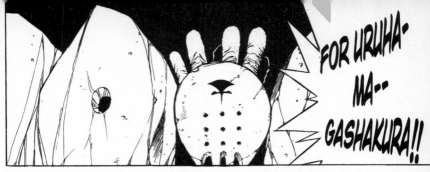

FOR URUHA-MA-- GASHAKURA!!

HE HAS NOT PARTICIPATED IN ANY PREVIOUS URABUTO-SATSUJIN! LIKE HOKAGE, HE IS AN UNKNOWN POWERHOUSE!!

GASHAKURA HAS WON FIVE STRAIGHT VICTORIES! HE DEFEATED FIVE OPPONENTS IN A ROW YESTERDAY!!

ALL RIGHT, MAGEN-SHA...

BEFORE YOU FIGHT...

A WORD WITH YOU, GASHAKURA.

WHAT KIND OF FIGHTER IS HE!?

WUSP

SO THAT'S GASHAKURA. HE'S HUGE!

WUSP

THEN THEY'LL PISS THEM-SELVES... WHEN THEY SEE THIS GUY FIGHT!!

HEH...THE GUYS IN BLOC A ARE FREAKING OUT.

*BEING CAST ADRIFT IN SPACE AND TIME.

FAREWELL...

SHOOK

SWOO

WHY'D YOU... WHERE'D THEY GO!?

MAGENSHA, WH-WHAT DID YOU DO!!?

RUSTLE

YA SEE THAT?

LIKE THE STRANGE WEAPON HE USED ON JISHO...

THAT GUY REALLY IS A MONSTER!!

THEIR POWERS WERE EXPOSED AND THEY LOST.

THEY GOT BETTER THAN THEY DESERVED.

MISTER HANABISHI...

KLAK KLAK

SHAKE SHAKE SHAKE SHAKE SHAKE

"HANABISHI!! SAVE SOME FOR THE REST OF US!!"

THOUGHT DOMON, WHO WAS SCHEDULED TO FIGHT MAGENSHA!!

SHALL WE BEGIN!?

G·LINK

ALL RIGHT, THE FUN'S OVER!

HUFF

HUFF

HMM?

I'M FIGHTIN' AGAIN!! GOT A PROBLEM WITH THAT?!

MY OPPONENT IS SOMEBODY CALLED FUKO!

YOU'RE STILL HERE? RUN ALONG, BOY!!

ALLOW ME TO EXPLAIN!

HEH, YOU CAN BARELY STAND UP...

I'M GOING NUMB... CAN'T MOVE...

WH-WHAT'S THIS!? MY BODY... FEELS WEIRD...

WHOOM

...

HE...HE...
MISSED
!!!

WHAT!?
RECCA'S
ALIVE!!!

SHE THREW HER LITTLE PICKS IN THE FIRST ROUND, TOO.

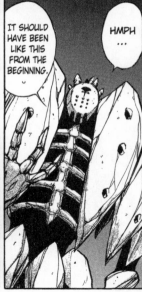

IT SHOULD HAVE BEEN LIKE THIS FROM THE BEGINNING.

HMPH
...

183

AND I HAVEN'T GOTTEN TO FIGHT SINCE FUJIMARU...

BUT I'M THE ONE THAT GUY WANTS!!

I'M REALLY LOOKING FORWARD TO THIS!

KLIK

FUKO OF THE FUJIN ...

...IS GONNA EXPLODE.

TO BE CONTINUED!!

MY PICTURE DIARY
EDGE
(STAFF VERSION)

"NOW DIE!"

SAME AGE AS SCHUMACHER

◀ ANIKI "BIG BROTHER" TAGUCHI ▶
FAVORITE PHRASE: "I'M JUST THINKING ABOUT ANZAI." (THEN DOES SOMETHING BAD)

◀ G.B. (GERMAN BAKA) YAMAMOTO ▶
FAVORITE PHRASE: "THE FIREARM'S DIRTY"

LEECH

◀ YASSY ▶
FAVORITE PHRASE: "HMPH," "HUFF"

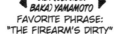

THEY ARE THE WARRIORS WHO BREATHE LIFE INTO "FLAME OF RECCA."

FLASH

ME

STOP! STOP!

FIGHT! FOR THE SAKE OF LOVE!!

FOR PEACE ON EARTH!!

IN MY SLEEP (TRUE STORY)

WHATEVER.

THE END

Spooky crimes, baffling robberies, and comic would-be detectives, no crime's too tough to crack for Jimmy! ... especially not his personal case: to find the mysterious masked men and make them change him back ... All the clues are here – can you solve the case before Jimmy does?

VOLUMES 1-15 OUT NOW!

find out more at www.orionbooks.co.uk

MEET JIMMY KUDO.

Ace high-school student with
keen powers of observation, he
helps police solve the baffling
crimes . . . until, hot on the trial
of a suspect, he's accosted and
fed a strange chemical which
transforms him into a puny
grade schooler!

COMPLETE OUR SURVEY AND
LET US KNOW WHAT YOU THINK!

❏ Please do NOT send me information about Gollancz Manga, or other Orion titles, products, news and events, special offers or other information.

Name: _____

Address: _____

Town: _____ County: _____ Postcode: _____

❏ Male ❏ Female Date of Birth (dd/mm/yyyy): ___/___/_____
(under 13? Parental consent required)

What race/ethnicity do you consider yourself? (please check one)

❏ Asian   ❏ Black   ❏ Hispanic

❏ White/Caucasian   ❏ Other: _____

Which Gollancz Manga series did you purchase?

❏ Case Closed   ❏ Dragon Ball   ❏ Dragon Ball Z ❏ Flame of Recca
❏ Fushigi Yûgi   ❏ Fushigi Yûgi: Genbu Kaiden   ❏ Maison Ikkoku
❏ One Piece   ❏ Rurouni Kenshin ❏ Yu-Gi-Oh!   ❏ Yu-Gi-Oh! Duelist

What other Gollancz Manga series have you tried?

❏ Case Closed   ❏ Dragon Ball   ❏ Dragon Ball Z ❏ Flame of Recca
❏ Fushigi Yûgi   ❏ Fushigi Yûgi: Genbu Kaiden   ❏ Maison Ikkoku
❏ One Piece   ❏ Rurouni Kenshin ❏ Yu-Gi-Oh!   ❏ Yu-Gi-Oh! Duelist

How many anime and/or manga titles have you purchased in the last year?
How many were Gollancz Manga titles?

Anime	Manga	GM
❏ None	❏ None	❏ None
❏ 1-4	❏ 1-4	❏ 1-4
❏ 5-10	❏ 5-10	❏ 5-10
❏ 11+	❏ 11+	❏ 11+

Reason for purchase: (check all that apply)
- ❏ Special Offer
- ❏ Favourite title
- ❏ Gift
- ❏ In store promotion If so please indicate which store: _____
- ❏ Recommendation
- ❏ Other _____

Where did you make your purchase?
- ❏ Bookshop
- ❏ Comic Shop
- ❏ Music Store
- ❏ Newsagent
- ❏ Video Game Store
- ❏ Supermarket
- ❏ Other: _____
- ❏ Online: _____

What kind of manga would you like to read?
- ❏ Adventure
- ❏ Comic Strip
- ❏ Fantasy
- ❏ Fighting
- ❏ Horror
- ❏ Mystery
- ❏ Romance
- ❏ Science Fiction
- ❏ Sports
- ❏ Other: _____

Which do you prefer?
- ❏ Sound effects in English
- ❏ Sound effects in Japanese with English captions
- ❏ Sound effects in Japanese only with a glossary at the back

Want to find out more about Manga?
Look it up at www.orionbooks.co.uk, or www.viz.com

THANK YOU!
Please send the completed form to:

Manga Survey
Orion Books
Orion House
5 Upper St Martin's Lane
London, WC2H 9EA

All information provided will be used for internal purposes only.
We promise not to sell or otherwise divulge your details.

NO PURCHASE NECESSARY. Requests not in compliance with all terms of this form will not be acknowledged or returned. All submissions are subject to verification and become property of Gollancz Manga.